Arbuckle Adventures

Jimmy's First Day Back to School

By: Cameron Williams

Arbuckle Adventures - Jimmy's First Day Back to School

Copyright © 2021 by Cameron Williams.
All rights reserved. No part of this book may be reproduced in any form or by any electronic or mechanical means, including information storage and retrieval systems, without permission in writing from the publisher, except by a reviewer who may quote brief passages in a review.

Arbuckle Adventures Series: Book #1

Self-Published by
Cameron Williams
Upper Marlboro, MD

ISBN: 978-1-7377779-0-8 (Paperback)

Library of Congress Control Number: 2021917130

Illustrations by
Jeck Flores

Book Cover and Interior Design by
Lysa Phillips of LPS Marketing Designs, LLC

Printed in the United States of America

First Printing Edition 2021

For more information, contact cameron231998@gmail.com

Dedication

This book and others in this series are dedicated to children around the world who want to experience joy, escape, comfort, and adventure the Arbuckle way. Reading this story, the young reader can connect with the character's journey and learn life lessons along the way. And for the adults, you'll get a glimpse of what children deal with as they navigate through their formative years.

Acknowledgment

I have learned that action is the key to achieving great things in life. As a result, God will provide the right people to help along the way. Thus, I give praise to God for blessing me with such a wonderful gift and revealing to me what my life's purpose is through prayer, receiving godly advice, and reading His word.

I am grateful to my parents, Andre and Millicent Williams, as well as my grandfather, Howard Cook, for their love, support, and encouragement.

Special thanks to the artist behind Jimmy Arbuckle, Jeck Flores, who brought my imagination to life with his talent unlike anyone I have known.

Moreover, it was a pleasure to work with Lysa Phillips from LPS Marketing Designs, LLC throughout the entire process, from cover design to interior design to publishing.

Jimmy's First Day Back to School

On a beautiful summer morning in Brooklyn, New York, 8-year-old Jimmy Arbuckle woke up from a deep sleep. Sitting upright in his bed, Jimmy heard his mom yelling out to him from downstairs, "Breakfast is ready!" Jimmy crawled out of bed, moving sluggishly to the kitchen.

Walking into the kitchen, Jimmy greeted his parents, who were seated at the table. "Wow, that's my favorite!" Jimmy said, gazing at the box of colorful, flavored cereal. It was everything any hungry child could ask for.

While Jimmy stuffed his mouth full of the delicious cereal, his dad asked in a deep but

gentle voice, "How are you feeling about going back to school and starting your first day of third grade, Jimmy?"

Lowering his head, Jimmy stopped eating and replied in a low, sad voice, "I would rather be home-schooled." Jimmy was not happy about starting a new school year. He did not want to go back.

His response surprised his parents. "I'm scared," he said. "Why are you scared?" they asked. "What if the other kids make fun of me? What if my teacher isn't nice and doesn't like me? What if I have trouble making friends? His mom and dad were overly concerned and sad when they heard his answer. It was important to them that he felt better. So, they started to encourage him. "You are very kind, Jimmy. The other boys and girls will like you and want to be your friend. You will make friends and have a good relationship with your teacher. You are a very smart young man. You can do it." They gave him hope and made him believe that entering third grade is not as bad as he thinks.

Jimmy and his parents cleared the dishes off the table after breakfast, and he and his dad went upstairs to get ready for the day, while his mom stayed behind to wash the dishes. With dazzling speed, the two of them came back downstairs fully dressed and ready to go. Jimmy and his dad headed to the car, got in, and drove away in a hurry. They did not want to be late on Jimmy's first day back to school.

Jimmy was enjoying the ride in the car, but he was getting nervous as they got closer to the school. His mind was filled with discouragement once again, wondering whether he would make new friends, if the work would be too difficult, or if he was going to get the worst teacher of all time. As soon as his dad noticed Jimmy's gloomy expression,

he turned on the radio to see if there was any song that could ease Jimmy's fears. Switching from station to station, he discovered one of their favorite songs by The Jackson 5, "ABC." The two of them were having a good ole' time singing along and having their own private concert, "ABC, it's easy as 1-2-3...."

When they finally arrived at Robinson Elementary School, Jimmy's dad noticed Jimmy was looking and feeling a lot better and still singing the "ABC" song even after the music had ended. In no time at all, Jimmy regained his confidence and was ready to make his first day the best day.

As they entered the school still humming the "ABC" song, they were surprised to see so many children and parents excited and energetic. Making their way through the crowd, Jimmy and his dad were drawn to a sign with an arrow that read, "Check-In: Cafeteria." So, off to the cafeteria they went.

"Dad, there are so many people here!" said Jimmy. At the cafeteria's entrance, they were greeted by a woman with long, blonde hair and a spunky attitude. "Welcome!" she said with excitement. "These are your son's enrollment forms. Please complete and return them to me." Moving at lightning speed, dad filled out the forms and returned them to her. She reviewed the forms and directed him to classroom 215 to meet Jimmy's new teacher.

While walking down the halls, Jimmy and his dad marveled at the bright, vibrant pictures of the faculty, students, and beautiful banners and paintings by each classroom.

They also spent time looking at the trophies in the trophy cases.

When they approached classroom 215, Jimmy's new teacher, Ms. Harrison, was standing at the door with a clipboard in hand filled with all the names of her students. She smiled as she welcomed Jimmy and his dad. Then she leaned forward and said, "Hello, you must be Jimmy. Welcome to your first day of third grade."

Thinking about what his son said earlier about returning to school, Jimmy's dad gently pulled him aside before he entered the classroom, hugged him tightly, and said, "Son, before you go in, I want to remind you of a few things. Do not be afraid to ask questions if you don't understand something. Don't be shy or afraid of your classmates and peers. They are here for the same reason you are. One last thing. This is very important. I love you." Jimmy smiled. "I love you too, dad," he said

as he walked into the classroom. Dad left for work hoping his son would have a great first day of school.

Although Jimmy had attended this school since kindergarten, the thought of entering third grade was a little scary for him. He recognized a couple of students from his second-grade class and saw many new faces he had never seen before. He sat at his desk, waiting for class to begin. After the morning

bell rang, Ms. Harrison stepped inside to take attendance. Seeing that everyone was present, she introduced herself and explained the rules of the classroom. She was tough, but a fair person who controlled her class and would not tolerate nonsense. Jimmy was impressed with Ms. Harrison and knew in his heart that he had the right teacher.

During the first half of class, Jimmy had a tough time staying focused. Suddenly he was bored and began daydreaming about fun things he had done during

the summer. Before he knew it, the bell rang. It was time for lunch. Jimmy was glad to get a break. "All right, students, let's get in line. No talking, no noises, and no getting out of line," Mrs. Harrison said in a soft but firm voice. Many of the students had trouble following the rules as they walked slowly to the cafeteria.

It seemed like it took them forever to get there. When the double doors opened automatically, Jimmy was surprised to see students from third to sixth grade sharing lunch, laughing, and enjoying each other's company.

Jimmy brought his lunch from home but waited for his entire class to receive their lunches so they could all eat together. As he waited patiently, Jimmy noticed a boy sitting alone on the far end of the table. So, he decided to walk over and introduce himself. "Hi! I'm Jimmy. May I sit here and eat lunch

with you?" Jimmy asked. "Sure, Jimmy. I don't mind at all. By the way, my name is Timothy," the boy replied. Even though Jimmy was a little nervous, he realized he took the first step towards making a new friend.

Jimmy sat next to Timothy. They ate lunch and talked about things that third-graders usually talk about. The two had a great time getting to know each other and finding out they had a lot in common. They enjoyed playing and watching sports, especially basketball. Both of them were into watching cartoons and travelling to fun places. Jimmy and Timothy were slowly but surely becoming good friends. Then, just before lunch ended, Jimmy leaned over to Timothy and asked if he would be interested in playing a game of one-on-one basketball during recess. "Yep, you bet!" Timothy replied.

The bell rang again, and the students knew what it meant. It was recess time! They were all excited. Everyone ran outside, not wasting a minute of fun. Several students played on the swing set, seesaw, monkey bars, and on the basketball court. Others played tag, jumped rope, and raced each other.

It was now time for Jimmy and Timothy's one-on-one match. Jimmy grabbed a basketball and called out to Timothy, "Hey, are you ready for our game?" Timothy rushed onto the court shouting, "Let's do this!" Hearts were pumping and pulses were racing as the boys showed off their skills. Both of them were dripping in sweat and breathing heavily.

Neither one of them wanted to lose the game.

Their pulse-pounding, competitive game drew the attention of other students who were on the playground. For Jimmy and Timothy, it was a glorious moment. With both having the same score, the pressure was on. Only one basket will determine the winner. With all eyes on them, the competition began. With the ball in his hands, Jimmy dribbles gracefully while slowing down. He gets past Timothy and takes his shot as soon as the administrator blows the whistle, forcing him to miss, hitting the rim of the hoop instead. Blowing of the whistle signaled the end of recess. Angry and upset that he did not make the shot, Jimmy demonstrated good sportsmanship and thanked Timothy for the great game.

The students lined up to head back inside the school building and into their classrooms. Back in Ms. Harrison's room, science was the last subject of the day—Jimmy's favorite. There was always something new he could learn. Sometimes it would be about the environment, sometimes it would be about nature, and other times it would be about outer space.

Drooling from the wonders of the amazing world of science, the blast of the final school bell brought Jimmy back to reality, letting him and the rest of the students know that the school day was over.

For many students, hearing the bell going off for dismissal was the best part of the day. Being around friends was good but getting to go home was even better.

"Goodbye, Timothy. It was nice meeting you," Jimmy said. "It was nice meeting you too. And by the way, next time, bring your 'A' game when we play basketball again," Timothy said jokingly. "Trust me, I will," Jimmy replied.

The two boys were incredibly excited; not because school was over, but because they had found a friend in the other on their first day of school.

THE END.